The Map Between Us

HE WAS HER DESTINATION. SHE WAS HIS ADVENTURE.

TREVOR JENSEN

Dedication

To the ones searching for their place in the story—who trace old maps, follow fading trails,and dare to write new endings when none seem left.

And to my father,whose stories taught me that memory is a kind of magic,and whose silences taught me that some truths wait to be found.

This book is for you.

Contents

Introduction

Maps don't always lead to places.

Sometimes, they lead to people.

To memories long buried.

To truths no one meant to uncover.

Jade Sinclair wasn't looking for a story when she found the map tucked inside her father's old field journal. She certainly wasn't looking for Logan Hale — the quiet mechanic with a past he won't talk about and eyes that see more than they let on.

But fate doesn't follow straight lines.

What begins as a simple cross-country road trip soon becomes something far stranger and more dangerous. Clues hidden in postcards. A feather that shouldn't exist. A message from someone who shouldn't know her name. Every mile forward unearths a secret fifteen years buried — and something, or someone, is following them.

This isn't just a journey.

It's a reckoning.

And the closer they get to the truth, the more Jade realizes:

Some stories don't want to be found.

Some maps weren't meant to be read.

And some hearts only find each other when everything else is falling apart.

Welcome to *The Map Between Us*.

Follow carefully.

The path is shifting.

And the story is watching.

Chapter 1: The Dare at Dusk

The last of the Tuesday sun bled through the grimy windows of The Rusty Mug, painting the dust motes in streaks of dying gold. It was the kind of light that made everything look either romantic or depressing, and lately, Jade Carter was leaning hard toward depressing. She slung a rag over her shoulder, the damp cloth a familiar weight, and surveyed her kingdom: a constellation of condensation rings on the dark wood of the bar, a trio of grizzled regulars nursing their IPAs, and the large **'FOR SALE'** sign planted in the bar's front lawn. It felt less like a real estate notice and more like a countdown timer on her life.

It was the smell that got to you after an eight-hour shift. Not the sharp, clean scent of citrus from the garnish tray, but the deeper, cloying perfume of stale beer that had seeped into the very soul of the floorboards.

"Another round for the history department?" Jade asked, her voice laced with the practiced cheer that paid her bills.

At the corner table, Logan Hayes didn't look up. He was staring at the trivia scorecard from last night as if it held the secrets to the universe. Which, in a way, it did. The final question, the one that had cost his team the win and the fifty-dollar bar tab prize, had been: *What explorer was killed in the Philippines after circumnavigating the globe?*

"Magellan," he muttered to his half-empty pint glass. "It was Magellan."

Jade smirked, though the expression didn't quite reach her eyes. "Tough break, Professor. Maybe next time."

She called him the Professor not because he was one—he was a high school history teacher, a fact the entire town of Harmony Creek seemed to know—but because he looked the part. Tweed-adjacent jacket even in the August heat, glasses that were perpetually sliding down his nose, and the quiet, observant air of a man who would rather read about life than live it. He was a fixture, a sad monument to Tuesday nights and what-if scenarios.

A gust of warm air and the jingle of the bell over the door announced the arrival of Ruby McCall. With her flame-red hair piled into a messy bun and a grin that promised trouble, Ruby was the human equivalent of a firecracker.

"Carter!" she boomed, sliding onto a stool at the bar. "Don't tell me you're going to spend the last days of this fine establishment memorizing the drinking habits of seventy-year-old men."

"It's a sociological study," Jade shot back, sliding a glass of water toward her. "And as long as this place is still open, it pays the rent."

"For now," Ruby said, her tone softening for a fraction of a second before her mischievous grin returned. "All the more reason to find some pirate gold, don't you think?" She leaned in, her voice dropping to a conspiratorial whisper. "I was cleaning out my grandma's attic. The box from your aunt Mae."

Jade's interest piqued. "The one with the cursed doll collection?"

"Better." Ruby's eyes glinted. She pulled a folded, brittle piece of paper from her back pocket.

The moment Jade saw the familiar, spidery handwriting, the air left her lungs. The cheerful mask she wore for customers dissolved. She'd know it anywhere.

"Ruby, where did you get that?" Her voice was sharp, stripped of its usual banter.

"Aunt Mae's box. She said it was your dad's." Ruby unfolded it gently on the bar, as if handling a holy relic. "His 'Map to a Better Place.' She said he was always drawing them. Said maybe it was time you saw it."

Jade stared at the faded ink on paper the color of weak tea. It wasn't just a map. It was a ghost. It depicted a winding route that seemed to start right here in the Midwest and snake its way southwest, marked with cryptic X's and his hand-scrawled notes: *"Where the sky meets the steel giant"* and *"Listen for the ghost's whisper."* A challenge from a man who had been more of a myth than a father.

Ruby, sensing the shift in the air, plowed ahead with the brazen confidence of a best friend who knew when to push. "This is a sign, Jade. The bar is closing, you have no plans... This is your chance. I dare you to actually *go* somewhere. Follow it."

Jade laughed, a short, sharp sound devoid of humor. "On what? Good intentions? I have responsibilities."

"You have a shift," Ruby corrected, her gaze flickering over Jade's shoulder to the solitary figure in the corner. An idea, brilliant and terrible, dawned on her face. "And you're not going alone."

Before Jade could protest, Ruby snatched the map and strode over to Logan's table. "Evening, Mr. Predictable," she said, her voice carrying across the quiet room.

Jade cringed, seeing Logan's shoulders tighten. The nickname, meant to be a playful jab, landed with the thud of a thrown rock. "Ruby, don't."

But Ruby was on a roll, slapping the map down next to the damning scorecard. "We're staging an intervention. Jade here needs to engage with her legacy, and you..." She paused. "You need to learn there's a world outside a history book. So, the dare is this: The two of you follow the map. Wherever it leads. You can't come back until you find the treasure."

Jade finally reached the table, her mind reeling. "She's kidding, Logan."

Logan's gaze was fixed on the map. He saw the pain in Jade's face, the desperate way she was trying to pretend this object wasn't a live wire. He saw the lines drawn by a hand he'd never known, leading to places he'd only dreamed of. Then he heard Ruby's word again. *Predictable.* It echoed the one his principal had used, the one that had been ringing in his ears for days.

His finger reached out, almost of its own accord, and traced one of the faded ink lines heading west. It was the most impulsive thing he'd done all year.

He lifted his head and looked at Jade, truly looked at her. He saw a woman holding a ghost in her hands, trying to pretend it wasn't heavy. He saw an escape hatch.

He took a slow breath. "Okay."

The word was so quiet, Jade almost missed it. "What?"

"I said okay," he repeated, his voice a low rumble of gravel and resolve. "I'll do it."

The silence in the bar was absolute. Ruby's jaw was slack.

Jade stared at him. This was not the plan. "You're serious?"

"Are you?" he countered.

Was she? A thousand voices screamed *no*. It was a reckless, stupid decision, the kind that had filled the little "regret jar" on her nightstand. But then she looked at her father's map, at Logan's face—the hurt now forged into something steely—and she knew her time in Harmony Creek was over one way or another.

"Fine," Jade said, the word tasting like freedom and panic. "But we do this right." She snagged a quarter from her jeans. "Call it. Heads, we leave at sunrise. Tails, we forget this happened and you get a beer on the house."

Logan watched the coin. "Heads."

Jade flicked it. The silver disc spun, catching the light before landing on the sticky tabletop with a clatter. It wobbled and settled. A perfect, gleaming head.

"Sunrise, then," Logan said, a ghost of a smile touching his lips. He stood, his six-foot frame seeming taller than it had moments before. He slid a ten-dollar bill onto the table. "For the beer."

Jade nodded, her throat suddenly dry. "Sunrise."

She extended a hand to seal the deal. His palm met hers. It was warm and surprisingly calloused, his grip firm. It wasn't the handshake of a man who only held books. A jolt went up her arm—not the flirty buzz of bar-side banter, but something deeper, a low hum of resonance. It lasted a beat too long before they let go.

Without another word, Logan turned and walked out, the bell over the door tinkling his departure.

Ruby let out a whoop. "I cannot believe that worked! The Professor's got some spine after all!"

From the end of the bar, Bob cleared his throat. "That boy's got more than spine. He's got his father's ghost sitting on his shoulder."

Jade paused, her hand halfway to collecting Logan's empty glass. "What are you talking about, Bob?"

Bob took a long sip of his stout. "His old man, Tom Hayes? Biggest risk-taker this county ever saw.

Climbed mountains, kayaked rapids... the works. Died in a rock-climbing accident up in the Sierras when Logan was just a boy. Tragic. His mother never recovered. Wrapped Logan in cotton wool ever since." He shook his head slowly. "That boy saying yes to a treasure map trip with you... that ain't just a dare, Jade. That's an earthquake."

The bar suddenly felt airless. The playful dare, the lucky coin flip, the thrilling handshake—it all curdled. The entire encounter shifted in Jade's mind. The quiet hurt in Logan's eyes, his steady resolve, tracing the line on the map... it wasn't the rebellion of a predictable man. It was the rebellion of a survivor.

And she, with her father's ghost in one hand and a dare in the other, had just handed him the dynamite.

She picked up the quarter from the table, its metallic coolness a stark contrast to the memory of his hand. She pocketed it. It didn't feel like another mistake destined for the regret jar. Not yet.

It felt like a key.

Chapter 2: The Pact is Sealed

The lock on Jade's apartment door clicked shut behind her, the sound unnervingly final. The cacophony of The Rusty Mug faded, replaced by the quiet hum of her own curated chaos. Her apartment was less a home and more a museum of good intentions and bad decisions. A stack of half-read philosophy books served as a coaster for a sweating glass of water. A chipped snow globe from a long-forgotten roadside stop sat next to a potted succulent that was valiantly clinging to life. And on her nightstand, glinting under the warm glow of a lava lamp, was the Regret Jar.

It was half full.

She dropped her keys into a ceramic bowl shaped like a grinning cat and walked straight to it. The quarter from the bar felt heavy in her pocket. For a moment, she considered it—writing *"Dared a grieving man into a cross-country existential crisis"* on a slip of paper and adding it to the collection. It would fit right in with *"Drove to Mardi Gras on a Tuesday and lost my car"* and *"Got a tattoo of a dolphin I thought was a shark."*

But Bob's words echoed in her ears. *That ain't just a dare, Jade. That's an earthquake.*

No, this felt different. This wasn't the familiar, fizzy thrill of recklessness. This was heavy. This was resonant. She left the quarter in her pocket. Taking a deep breath, she pulled her father's map from her bag and spread it across the worn wood of her kitchen table. The lines he'd drawn were confident, sweeping strokes of a man who believed the world was his to chart. *His Map to a Better Place.* What a joke. His better place had been the bottom of a bottle, leaving her and Aunt Mae to navigate the wreckage. A familiar anger, hot and sharp, pricked at her.

As if summoned by the thought of family, her phone screen lit up with a text from Aunt Mae.

Aunt Mae: Ruby called me. Said you took the bait.

Jade rolled her eyes, but a warmth spread through her chest.

Jade: It was a coin flip. Could've gone either way.

Aunt Mae: Honey, with one of your father's maps, the coin is always rigged. Be safe.

Before Jade could reply, her phone buzzed again, vibrating against the table with a startling intensity. An unknown number.

Her heart gave a painful lurch. It had to be him. She swiped to answer, pitching her voice into a casual, breezy tone she was nowhere near feeling. "Talk to me."

"Jade? It's, uh, Logan. Hayes."

His voice was exactly as she remembered it—a quiet, deliberate rumble. But over the phone, it felt more intimate, like a secret whispered in the dark.

"Professor," she said, forcing a lightness. "Having second thoughts? Realize you forgot to catalogue your sock drawer for the summer?"

There was a beat of silence on his end, and then, to her complete surprise, a dry chuckle. "My mother thinks it's a suicide mission," he said, his voice losing its formal edge for a moment. "I figured a military invasion was a good compromise."

Jade froze, a smirk tugging at her lips. The honesty of it—the unexpected flash of dark humor—was completely disarming. It was the first thing he'd said that didn't sound rehearsed. "Right," she said, her own voice softening. "Compromise is key in any successful suicide mission."

"Exactly," he said, and she could almost hear him smile. "So, I've packed a supply of non-perishable snacks, a water purification filter, and a comprehensive first-aid kit. I also have a travel edition of Catan, in case we're... you know. Stranded."

She sank onto a kitchen chair, the weight of his words landing squarely on her chest. He was trying to control the uncontrollable, to plan away the possibility of tragedy. Every item he listed was a prayer against the ghost on his shoulder.

"And what, exactly, are you bringing to the table?" he asked, the defensiveness back in his voice.

Jade looked at the duffel bag she'd thrown on the floor. "My winning personality, a bag of gas station jerky, and this map. The essentials."

"Right," he said, the single word conveying a universe of doubt. "Jade... are you sure about this? It's not too late."

He was giving her an out. The responsible part of her screamed to take it. But the other part, the part that now knew Aunt Mae had rigged the coin, knew she couldn't. "I'm sure, Logan," she said. "Are you?"

She heard him exhale, a shaky breath of air. "Yes. I am."

"Okay then," she said, a new resolve hardening inside her. "My place. 6 a.m. Don't be late, Professor. The horizon waits for no man."

"I won't," he said, and hung up.

Jade stared at her phone, her heart hammering. Her phone immediately buzzed again with a series of texts.

Ruby: RULE #1: NO TURNING BACK. **Ruby:** RULE #2: PROFESSOR HAYES IS NOT ALLOWED TO USE A SPREADSHEET. **Ruby:** RULE #3: IF YOU DON'T MAKE OUT IN A CORNFIELD AT LEAST ONCE I WILL HAVE FAILED AS YOUR FRIEND.

A real, genuine laugh escaped her, breaking the tension. She typed back a single, profane emoji and tossed her phone onto the couch. Time to pack.

She moved with purpose, stuffing clothes into her duffel. Boots, shorts, souvenir t-shirts. Then came the talismans: a copy of *On the Road* with a cracked spine and a small, smooth river rock. She pulled out a notepad and scribbled on a fresh sheet. *For Dad, and for Tom Hayes. Find what you were both looking for.* She folded it into a tight square and tucked it deep inside her wallet.

Her bag was packed. One last look. She picked up the map to place it in her bag. Her fingers brushed over a section near the top, and she paused. It felt... thick. A crease that didn't quite match the others.

Working her thumbnail carefully under the edge, she gently pried it open. Tucked inside the hidden flap was a small, square photograph, its colors faded to a dreamy sepia.

It was her. Six or seven years old, gap-toothed, squinting against a brilliant sun. She was standing in front of a landmark she didn't recognize—a bizarre, towering sculpture of welded metal that looked like a giant, skeletal bird. In the bottom right corner of the frame, a man's thumb was partially visible. Her father's thumb.

Jade sank onto the floor, her legs suddenly weak. She stared at the image, searching her memory for a flicker of recognition, but found only a blank wall. Her eyes darted from the photo back to the map spread on her table. Her gaze fell on the first X, the first destination. The spidery handwriting next to it read: ***"Where the sky meets the steel giant."***

A cold dread, mingled with an electric thrill, washed over her. It wasn't a coincidence. Her father hadn't just drawn a map to some random place. He had drawn a map back to this photo. Back to this memory.

The first stop wasn't just a dot on a page. It was a question about her own life she now desperately needed to answer.

Chapter 3: Detours and Daydreams

Dawn in Harmony Creek was less a sunrise and more a slow leaking of grey into the black sky. At precisely 0559, a pair of headlights cut through the morning mist and pulled up to Jade's apartment building. It wasn't the sensible sedan she'd pictured, but a dark green, slightly battered Jeep Wrangler that looked like it had stories to tell. It was clean, she noted, but the dents and scratches were worn like badges of honor.

Logan killed the engine. He was a silhouette in the driver's seat. Waiting.

Jade slung her duffel bag over her shoulder, took one last look at her apartment, and locked the door behind her. This was it. The earthquake was beginning.

"Morning, Professor," she said, tossing her bag into the back. It landed with a lumpy thud next to a set of perfectly organized, military-grade storage containers. "You're punctual. I'm shocked."

"Punctuality is a form of preparedness," he said, his eyes scanning her—her messy pixie cut, her faded band t-shirt, the nervous energy humming off her like static. "Ready?"

"Born ready," she lied, sliding into the passenger seat. The cab of the Jeep was surprisingly spacious but undeniably intimate. The air smelled of clean vinyl and strong coffee from the battered travel mug in his center console. His hand was resting on the gear shift, and she was acutely aware of the proximity of his knee to hers.

He turned the key, and the engine rumbled to life. As he pulled away from the curb, a tinny, instrumental track began to play—something orchestral and inspiring, like the soundtrack to a nature documentary.

Jade stared at the stereo. "What is this? 'Triumphant Journeys of the American Bald Eagle'?"

A faint blush crept up Logan's neck. "It's a motivational playlist. Studies show that goal-oriented music can increase efficiency."

"Right." Before he could react, Jade leaned over, her arm brushing his, and plugged her phone into the auxiliary jack. The soaring orchestra was immediately murdered by the raw, chaotic opening chords of a 90s garage rock anthem.

Logan flinched but didn't protest. He just gripped the steering wheel, a small, tight smile on his face, and drove them out of town as the sun began to break over the horizon.

The first hour was a study in awkward silence. Jade watched the familiar landscape of her life recede in the side mirror, her stomach a knot of anxiety. Suddenly, a violent *thump-wump-wump* erupted from the front passenger side, and the Jeep lurched sickeningly.

"I believe the technical term is a flat tire," Jade said, already unbuckling her seatbelt as Logan expertly guided the vehicle to the dusty shoulder.

He, the man of a thousand plans, looked momentarily lost. This was an unscheduled event. Jade, meanwhile, felt a strange sense of calm. She hopped out into the shimmering heat and gave the shredded tire a professional kick. "Yep. She's a goner."

They fell into an odd, bickering rhythm as they worked. He'd read a step from the owner's manual, and she'd tell him she was already doing it. They worked in close quarters, a dance of bumped elbows and brushed hands. Just as they were tightening the last nut, a rusty pickup truck slowed behind them. An older man in a greasy cap leaned out.

"Your little lady know what she's doing with that thing?" he drawled, nodding at the tire iron in her hand.

Jade's back stiffened. Before she could unleash her sarcasm, Logan stepped slightly in front of her. "She knows exactly what she's doing," he said, his voice calm, level, and utterly non-negotiable. "But we appreciate the offer."

The man grunted, rolled up his window, and sped off. Jade stared at Logan, speechless. He turned back to the tire as if nothing had happened.

"You good?" he asked, not looking at her.

"Yeah," she said, her voice quieter than usual. "I'm just... used to fighting my own battles."

He finally looked up at her, his expression unreadable. "You don't have to," he said simply. "Not this one." And then he went back to work, leaving Jade to grapple with the strange, unsettling feeling of having someone in her corner.

An hour later, they arrived. The sculpture park rose from the sun-baked plains like a fever dream. And there, in the center of it all, was the giant. It was a skeletal, bird-like creature of welded steel, just as bizarre and imposing as it was in the photograph. Jade's heart hammered against her ribs.

She walked toward it as if in a trance, leaving Logan behind with the map. She reached out a trembling hand and laid it flat against the sun-warmed, rusted steel. Closing her eyes, she tried to summon something—a sound, a feeling, the ghost of a gap-toothed grin. Anything. Nothing came but the metallic smell of the rust and the heat on her palm.

"Hey, are you okay?" Logan's voice was soft, close behind her.

Her eyes snapped open. "Yeah, fine," she said, pulling her hand back quickly. "Just... taking in the artistic majesty."

Logan gave her a curious look, a slight frown between his brows. "Right. You seem... elsewhere."

"It's very moving art," she deflected, turning her back on the sculpture before he could see the lie in her eyes. "Come on, let's find that shadow."

At precisely noon, the giant's shadow stretched out, its tip landing on a small maintenance plaque at the base of a nearby sculpture. Taped to the back was a small, waterproof pouch. Inside wasn't a key, but something far stranger: a tarnished silver pocket compass. Jade opened it. The needle spun erratically, pointing nowhere near north. It was broken.

"Well, that's helpful," she muttered.

"Wait, turn it over," Logan said.

Etched onto the back in her father's familiar scrawl was a riddle: ***"Where the Storm King sleeps, find the heart of the stone."***

"Okay," Logan said, a genuine, triumphant grin spreading across his face. "I'd say this calls for a celebratory milkshake."

They found a diner ten miles down the road, a perfect time capsule of cracked red vinyl and chrome. Sliding into a booth, the adrenaline and exhaustion finally hit.

"I have to ask," Logan said, stirring his shake with his straw. "What's the story with your dad? Was he always like this? Creating these elaborate games?"

Jade's cheerful demeanor faltered for just a second. She watched a drop of condensation trail down her glass. "He was good at starting adventures," she said carefully, choosing her words from a place of long practice. "The beginnings were always magical. He wasn't always so good at… finishing them."

Logan seemed to hear the volumes left unsaid in her statement. He nodded slowly, a new understanding dawning in his eyes. "Well," he said, tapping the broken compass on the table between them. "Let's prove him wrong. Let's finish this one."

A warmth bloomed in her chest, chasing away some of the shadows. Maybe he was right. She pulled out the map to decipher the riddle. "'Where the Storm King sleeps...'" she read aloud.

Logan pointed to a jagged range of hills on the map. "There. The locals call it Storm King's Peak."

As he said the name, Jade's gaze drifted out the diner window. In the distance, the sun was beginning its slow descent, setting fire to the clouds. But it was setting behind a dark, jagged line of hills that rose ominously from the plains. And far beyond them, the sky was bruised with the unmistakable, turbulent purple-grey of gathering storm clouds.

Storm King's Peak. The name and the view collided in her gut with a sudden, chilling sense of foreboding. The easy part was over. The real journey was just about to begin.

Chapter 4: The Hill and the Heart

The celebratory mood of the diner evaporated the moment they got back in the Jeep. The sky ahead was a dramatic, bruised canvas of purple and grey, and the wind had picked up, rocking the vehicle in sharp, sudden gusts. The setting sun was a desperate, fiery slash on the horizon, a light they were quickly losing.

"The heart of the stone," Logan said, his voice tight with focus. He drove with a new, controlled intensity, his eyes fixed on the jagged silhouette of the hills ahead. "It could be a geode. Or a carving. Or it could be a metaphor."

"My dad wasn't big on metaphors," Jade said, turning the cool, broken compass over in her hands. "He was big on games. This is a game." She looked at the ominous peaks growing larger in the windshield. "One with a time limit."

A low, guttural rumble of thunder vibrated through the floor of the Jeep. This wasn't a race for a milkshake anymore. This was a race against the storm.

They reached the base of the largest hill as the last vestiges of sunlight were being swallowed by the clouds. A crude, barely-there trail snaked upwards into the dusk.

"We go on foot from here," Logan said, pulling the emergency brake.

They jumped out, the wind whipping Jade's hair across her face. It smelled of rain and damp earth. Adrenaline, sharp and electric, surged through her veins. Looking up at the steep, treacherous incline, a familiar, reckless impulse took over.

"Race you to the top!" she yelled over the wind. "Last one there has to tell their most embarrassing secret!"

Logan's face hardened, the playful energy between them vanishing. "Don't be stupid, Jade," he snapped, his voice sharp and cold. "This isn't a game. People get hurt acting reckless on terrain like this."

The harshness of his tone hit her like a slap. "Fine," she shot back, stung. "Be careful. I'll send you a postcard from the top."

She turned and scrambled up the first ledge without looking back, the thrill of the race now mixed with the bitter taste of anger. She climbed fast, fueled by a need to prove him wrong. When she glanced back, Logan was behind her, moving with a methodical, pained caution.

She summited first, breathless and triumphant. The view was terrifyingly magnificent. The storm front was a colossal, moving wall, flashes of lightning illuminating its depths. Logan hauled himself over the final ledge a moment later, his breathing ragged. He stood a safe distance from the edge, his back to the vista.

"What took you so long, Professor?" Jade teased, the anger still clinging to her. "Worried you'd have to confess you still sleep with a nightlight?"

He didn't answer. He was staring at his own feet, his jaw tight.

"Logan?"

"I'm not great with heights," he finally admitted, the words clipped.

And just like that, her anger dissolved, replaced by a wave of sharp, potent empathy. It wasn't about her. It was the ghost on his shoulder.

She walked over to him, her movements slow. "Hey," she said softly. He finally looked at her. "Don't look down. Look at me." His hazel eyes, wide with a vulnerability he couldn't hide, locked on hers. "Just breathe. We're on solid ground."

She took a small step back. "Now, just... turn. Slowly. Keep your eyes on me."

He trusted her. He pivoted, his body rigid. As he turned, his boot skidded on a patch of loose gravel. He flinched back with a sharp intake of breath, but Jade's reflexes were instant. She shot her hand out, grabbing his forearm. Her grip was strong, anchoring him.

"I've got you," she said, her voice low and certain.

He looked from her hand on his arm back to her eyes, his own wide with a startled mix of fear and gratitude. He nodded, and she let go. He was steady now. The real test was over.

"Now," she said gently. "The heart of the stone."

They scanned the rocky summit and found it: a single, distinctive stone shaped unmistakably like a heart. Prying it from its earthy socket, they found a small, rusted metal lockbox nestled beneath.

Logan lifted the lid. Inside were two objects: a folded, yellowed piece of notepaper, and a vintage, tarnished souvenir token. Jade picked up the token. It was cool and heavy in her palm, depicting a cluster of crystals under the words *THE CRYSTAL CAVERNS*. As her fingers closed around it, a phantom sensation shot through her—the sudden, jarring feeling of cold, damp air on her skin and the faint, echoing sound of dripping water. It was gone as quickly as it came, leaving her with a dizzying sense of *déjà vu*. She shook her head, unsettled, and turned her attention to the note.

She unfolded it. The note read:

The real test isn't the climb. It's trusting someone to catch you. - T.C.

The words hung in the charged air, made real by the moment that had just passed. They sat on the rocks, the wind dying down for a strange, breathless moment. The light from the setting sun and the approaching storm created an ethereal glow. A slow, unguarded smile spread across Logan's face—a look of pure relief and wonder.

Acting on pure instinct, she pulled out her phone and, through the screen, framed his face against the magnificent, stormy sky. She snapped the picture.

The soft *click* of the shutter was barely audible over the wind, but he heard it. His smile faded as he turned, his gaze questioning. "What was that?"

Jade's heart leaped into her throat. She fumbled with her phone, shoving it into her pocket. "Nothing," she said, her voice coming out a little too high. "You had... a storm cloud on your face. A smudge. It's gone now."

He didn't look convinced. He just held her gaze, and in that moment, the air was more charged than the storm clouds above them. She was someone who saw him, and he was someone who knew he was being seen.

Ping.

The first fat drop of rain hit the metal lockbox, the sound as loud as a gunshot in the sudden silence.

It was followed by a brilliant, blinding flash of lightning that bleached the world white for a second, and then a deafening, ground-shaking *CRACK* of thunder that felt like it was right on top of them.

The sky opened. The storm wasn't coming anymore. It was here. And they were on the highest point for miles, completely exposed, as the heavens broke apart.

Chapter 5: Storm Shelter

The world exploded into water and wind. The first deluge was a solid, blinding sheet, turning the air, the ground, and the sky into a single, roaring entity.

"Down!" Logan yelled, his voice nearly ripped away by the gale. "We have to get down now!"

Survival instinct obliterated everything else. It was all stripped away, leaving only the primal need to not die on this forsaken hill. The descent was a controlled fall. The trail had dissolved into a slick, muddy torrent. Logan, the man who was afraid of heights, was suddenly a rock. He grabbed Jade's hand, his grip like a vise. "Stay with me!" he shouted over the thunder.

They half-ran, half-slid down the treacherous path, working as a single unit. He'd brace his feet and anchor her; she'd find a path he couldn't see. They tumbled the last few feet to the bottom and scrambled for the Jeep, falling inside and slamming the doors shut against the fury of the storm.

For a long moment, there was no sound but the deafening drumming of rain on the roof and their own ragged gasps for air. Logan put his hands on the steering wheel to start the car, but they were shaking violently, a delayed reaction to the adrenaline. Without thinking, Jade reached across the center console and placed her hand over his.

"Hey," she said softly. "We're okay."

Her touch was steady, a small patch of warmth in the cold, damp car. He took a shuddering breath, turned his hand over, and squeezed her fingers once—a brief, desperate gesture of thanks. Then he pulled away, his hands now steady, and started the engine.

Through the deluge, a flickering, sickly green neon sign sputtered to life: S_E_PY C_CTUS M_TEL.It was the most beautiful thing she'd ever seen.

The man at the desk gave them the last room—two double beds, take it or leave it. They took it.

The room was a time capsule of wood-paneled walls and a threadbare orange carpet. As they navigated the awkwardness of divvying up the bathroom, Jade's eyes landed on a faded, tacky painting of a lone ship on a stormy sea, bolted to the wall.

"Subtle," she muttered, nodding toward the artwork. "Very on-theme for the evening."

Logan looked at it, a strange expression on his face. "My mom has one just like it in her hallway," he said quietly. "She bought it after my dad died. Says it reminds her that the smartest place for any ship is safe in the harbor."

The words settled between them, heavy with meaning. Jade looked from the sad, lonely painting to Logan and understood a little more about the cage he was trying to break out of.

After they had both changed into dry clothes, the single bulb in the ceiling flickered and died. The neon sign outside went dark. They were plunged into absolute blackness.

"Stay put," Logan's voice said. A zipper, and then a powerful beam of light cut through the dark. He placed the flashlight on the table between the beds, aiming it at the ceiling. It cast a soft, ambient glow, creating an isolated island of light in the vast, stormy darkness.

"Your most embarrassing secret," Jade prompted, sitting on the edge of her bed. "You lost the race."

He actually smiled. "When I was ten, I tried to mummify my hamster, Nibbles, with toilet paper and salt. My mom found it. I was grounded for a month."

Jade's genuine, unrestrained laugh felt like a release, and it broke the dam. The darkness made confession easy.

He told her about his dream of designing a board game. "In a game, there are rules," he explained, his voice low. "You can strategize. You can control the outcome, or at least understand why you lost. It's... safe. Real life isn't like that."

Jade, feeling a surge of trust, found herself talking about her blog. "My dad collected places. I guess I'm collecting the stories that go with them," she admitted. "Trying to figure out if his maps lead anywhere good, or if they only ever lead... away. I want to prove that running towards something is different."

"I think you already are," he said, his voice soft.

The conversation lulled, the space between them filled with a new, fragile intimacy. In a gesture of pure gratitude, Jade reached out, intending to just briefly touch his hand. At the exact same moment, he reached for her.

Their fingers brushed, hovering in the charged, electric space between the two beds. The contact sent a jolt straight through her system. The world narrowed to the few inches of space between their hands. Then, as if zapped by the same current, they both pulled back.

"Well," Logan cleared his throat, his voice suddenly husky. "We should probably get some sleep."

"Yeah," Jade breathed, her heart racing. "Goodnight, Logan."

"Goodnight, Jade."

She turned away, lying in the strange bed, in the strange room, acutely aware of the sound of his breathing just a few feet away. She replayed the near-touch, the spark, the silent, aborted question.

Her phone, which she'd plugged in before the power died, buzzed weakly on the nightstand. It had just enough battery. Thinking it was Ruby, she picked it up.

It was a picture—a grainy screenshot of a local newspaper article from fifteen years ago. The headline read: LOCAL MAN MISSING NEAR STORM KING'S PEAK.The accompanying photo was of a smiling, familiar man. Her father.

Below it, Ruby's text message glowed in the dark.

Ruby: Jade... was looking up stuff about your dad for fun. You need to see this. Is this what you're doing? Please be careful.

The air in Jade's lungs turned to solid ice. The phone slipped from her numb fingers, clattering softly onto the thin carpet. A wave of nausea washed over her. This wasn't a game. This wasn't a whimsical adventure.

It was a cold case. An unsolved mystery.

She looked across the dark room at Logan's sleeping form, at the gentle rise and fall of his chest. He was a good man, a man she had pulled from his safe harbor into the heart of her family's private tragedy without even knowing it.

And worse, as her thoughts spun, another image returned. Not the newspaper clipping—but a foggy memory. A voice from years ago, from her aunt Mae's porch, muttering after too much gin.

"Someone else was up there. Not a storm. Not an accident. He wasn't alone."

Jade had never asked questions. She'd assumed it was just grief talking.

But now... now it felt like a warning.

The map wasn't a gift from her father. It was a trail someone else might already be following.

And now, she was carrying it straight into their hands.

Chapter 6: Diner Confessions

Sleep never came. Jade lay awake in the dark, the sound of Logan's steady breathing from the other bed a counter-rhythm to the frantic pounding of her own heart. The storm outside had dwindled to a gentle, cleansing rain, but a far more violent storm was raging inside her.

LOCAL MAN MISSING NEAR STORM KING'S PEAK.

The words were seared onto the back of her eyelids. This wasn't a whimsical adventure. It was a cold case.

She slipped out of bed as the first hint of grey dawn seeped through the window. She watched Logan sleep, the anxious lines on his face smoothed out, and a wave of protective guilt washed over her. She had to tell him. It was the only right thing to do. But the selfish, desperate part of her was terrified to be alone with this darkness.

They packed in a strained, fragile silence.

They found a diner down the road, a bubble of cheerful neon and the warm, welcoming smell of coffee and bacon. They slid into a booth, the vinyl cool against her skin. The waitress came and went, leaving them with two steaming mugs of coffee and plates of food. Logan took a grateful sip of his coffee. Jade just stared at hers, her hands trembling so slightly she hoped he wouldn't notice. The secret was a physical weight, pressing down on her, making it hard to breathe.

"You're a million miles away," Logan said softly, his voice cutting through her internal chaos. "Where'd you go?"

"Nowhere," she lied, forcing a smile that felt brittle. "Just tired."

He didn't look convinced. He watched her for a long moment, his gaze full of a knowing gentleness. "I know that look," he said. "The one where you're trying to hold the entire world on your shoulders so no one sees the cracks. For me, it always comes back to my dad."

He stared into his coffee cup. "He used to say, 'A ship in harbor is safe, but that is not what ships are built for.' My mom, though..." he continued, a sad smile touching his lips. "She bought a painting of a ship in a storm after he died. Hung it in the hallway. Says it reminds her that the smartest place for any ship is safe in the harbor. That's the real reason I never left Harmony Creek."

He finally met her eyes, and the confession she'd been dreading and craving all night came pouring out.

"After he died, she... she collapsed. And I felt like it was my job to hold her together. I had to be responsible. I had to be safe. Every time I even thought about leaving, I'd see the panic in her eyes. The terror that she was going to lose me, too. Staying put stopped being about my fear and started being about hers. It felt like... my responsibility to not cause her any more pain. Leaving feels like the ultimate betrayal."

He spoke with a quiet, devastating honesty. Jade just listened. She didn't offer a single platitude. She just witnessed it. She saw the crushing weight of the legacy he carried, and in it, she felt the sharp, painful echo of her own.

When he was finished, the air between them was raw, but clean. He looked lighter. Seen.

To break the heavy, sacred silence, Jade reached into her pocket and slid the tarnished token for The Crystal Caverns across the table.

"Your turn," she said softly. "You choose what's next. You make the call."

He stared at the token, then at her. A slow, dawning understanding filled his eyes. He was being trusted. He picked up the token, pulled out his phone, and made the call, his voice clear and steady as he asked about hours of operation. When he hung up, he looked at her father's broken compass still sitting on the table and gave a wry shake of his head.

"Well, this thing is officially useless," he said, nudging the tarnished silver with his finger.

"Then here's one that works," Jade said. She grabbed a paper napkin and, with a few quick strokes of a borrowed pen, drew a simple, stylized compass. She pushed it across the table. "It only points in one direction," she told him. "Forward."

He looked down at the hand-drawn compass, then up at her, and his smile was breathtakingly grateful. "Thanks, Jade." He picked up his phone to put it away.

Just then, it buzzed violently on the table, the sound an aggressive intrusion. The screen lit up, illuminating his face.

The caller ID read: **MOM**.

Jade watched as his smile vanished instantly, replaced by a look of pure, cornered dread. The safe harbor was calling, its foghorn blasting, trying to pull its last ship home. As he stared at the screen, paralyzed, Jade's own phone, lying face down on the seat beside her, vibrated with a soft buzz.

She knew without looking who it was. A follow-up text from Ruby. A demand for an answer. A reminder of the missing man, the cold case, the ghost on the mountain.

They sat there, frozen in the cheerful diner, each held captive by a different call from a world they were desperately trying to escape.

Chapter 7: Horizons Unfolding

The cheerful clatter of the diner faded into a dull roar. The world narrowed to the two glowing screens on the table, two portals to the pasts they were trying to outrun. Jade watched Logan, his face a battlefield. This was it. The safe harbor or the open sea.

With a slow, deliberate movement that felt more definitive than any word, he pressed the power button on the side of his phone. The screen went black. He shoved the dark, silent phone into his pocket.

He looked up at her, his eyes wild with a potent mix of terror and exhilaration. "The Crystal Caverns," he said, his voice a little shaky but resolved. "That's what the token said, right?"

Just then, her own phone buzzed on the seat, a text preview from Ruby flashing on the screen: JADE. Are you okay??

Logan nodded toward it. "What about yours? Sounds important."

Jade's heart hammered. She looked down at the screen, at the silent scream from her best friend, at the ghost of her father trapped behind the glass. Then she looked up at Logan's face, at the terrified hope there. She couldn't break him. Not now.

She flipped the phone over, the screen going dark. "It can wait," she said, her voice miraculously steady. "Nothing's more important than this."

The lie settled between them, a foundation of stone and sand.

The drive away from the diner was different. The air was charged, purposeful. The sun was fully out now, the post-storm world so bright and clean it almost hurt to look at. They didn't talk about the phone calls. It was a silent pact.

They found The Crystal Caverns an hour later. It was a perfect slice of vintage roadside Americana, complete with a giant, twenty-foot-tall sculpture of a cartoonish prospector holding a massive, glittering crystal.

"There's no way the clue is just sitting in the cave with the rest of the tourists," Jade said, an idea sparking. She hopped out of the Jeep, pulling the bandana from her hair. "I bet it's out here. And you have to find it... blind."

"Jade, this is ridiculous," he said, but he didn't pull away as she gently tied the soft fabric over his eyes.

"The world is full of ridiculous things," she whispered, her voice close to his ear. "That's the fun part." She took his hand. His fingers were stiff at first, then slowly relaxed, lacing with hers.

She led him forward, her voice his only guide. "Okay, gravel beneath your feet. To your left is the smell of over-priced popcorn."

The physical contact was constant, a warm, steady current between them. He was completely reliant on her. His hand tightened on hers.

"It's weird," he said, his voice quiet and wondering.

"What is?"

"I can't see a thing," he admitted. "But I feel... safer than I did on that hill."

The admission hung in the air, a fragile, beautiful thing. It settled in Jade's chest, a warmth that fought against the cold knot of her secret.

She led him to the base of the giant prospector sculpture. "Okay," she said. "I think we're here. Use your other senses."

He let go of her hand and reached out, his fingers tracing the plaster base. "There are indentations," he murmured. "Letters. It feels like a code."

He pulled off the blindfold, blinking in the bright sunlight. He stared at the string of letters, a triumphant gleam in his eyes. His teacher brain fired up. "It's a simple substitution cipher," he said, a thrill in his voice. He scribbled on the back of their diner receipt. In a few minutes, he had it. "'At the heart of the falls, a new direction waits.' It's the next clue."

"See?" she said, bumping his shoulder with hers. "Told you you had a big brain."

He looked at her, his face flushed with pride and excitement. "We're a good team," he said, and the way he said it made her heart do a little flip.

They were laughing, high on their victory, the world feeling full of infinite, sun-drenched possibility. His phone buzzed in his pocket. He pulled it out, his good mood faltering slightly as he glanced at the screen.

"Who is it?" Jade asked.

He looked at the screen, and his face changed—not with dread this time, but with a complicated mix of surprise and annoyance. "My old college friend, Tyler," he said, the name sounding like an unwelcome memory on his tongue.

"A good friend?"

Logan let out a short, humorless laugh. "He's the guy I used to plan road trips with," he said, his gaze distant. "The ones I never had the guts to actually go on. He went on all of them." He looked back at his phone, his thumb hovering over the screen. "He says he's in the area. Wants to know if we want to grab a beer."

Chapter 8: The Rival and the Reveal

Logan stared at the text message, the cheerful chaos of the tourist stop fading into a dull hum. Tyler. The name itself was an echo from another life—a time of almosts and not-quites, of routes imagined but never taken.

"A good friend?" Jade asked again, her voice soft.

Logan let out a short, humorless laugh. "He's the guy I used to plan road trips with," he said, the admission tasting like old regret. "The ones I never had the guts to actually go on. He went on all of them."

He looked at Jade, at her bright, curious eyes, and a familiar wave of insecurity washed over him. She wouldn't understand. People like her did things. People like him planned them. Until now.

"We don't have to," Jade said gently, reading the hesitation on his face.

But the thought of hiding felt like a step backward. "No," he said, forcing a confidence he didn't feel. "It's just a beer. It'll be fine."

They met at a summer street fair that was a wall of sensory overload: the sticky-sweet smell of cotton candy, the chaotic symphony of carnival music, the press of the crowd. And then there was Tyler—six feet of effortless charm and too-white teeth, clapping Logan on the back with a force that nearly knocked him off balance.

"Hayes, you son of a gun!" Tyler boomed, before turning his high-wattage smile on Jade. "And you must be the accomplice. Tyler Benson."

His eyes lingered on Jade a beat too long. Not a leer, exactly—more a calculated assessment. Jade stiffened.

The whole hour was a masterclass in Tyler's passive aggression. He'd bring up their old plans—"Remember that cross-country trip to see the Redwoods, Lo? I ended up going with Sarah, you would have loved it"—and then turn to Jade, positioning himself as the real adventurer, the one who followed through.

To Jade, it all sounded familiar. Too familiar.

He reminded her of her father.

All stories. All charisma. All movement.

And always leaving someone behind.

They passed a knock-down-the-clowns carnival game. "My treat!" Tyler announced, swaggering up to win a prize for Jade and missing spectacularly. "Rigged," he declared with a wink.

"My turn," Jade said, her voice sharper than before. She stepped up and, with a precise flick of her wrist, sent the entire pyramid of clowns collapsing.

"We have a winner!" the attendant shouted.

Tyler pointed to a giant, garish purple bear. "There you go, Jade."

Jade ignored him. She pointed to a small, goofy-looking stuffed bat with one wing slightly askew. She grabbed it and, turning her back completely on Tyler, held it out to Logan.

"For the dashboard," she said softly. "To ward off bad spirits."

The gratitude in Logan's eyes was so profound it almost buckled her knees. It was a public declaration. I'm with him.

The shift was immediate. Tyler, sidelined, dropped the friendly façade.

"You know, Logan," he said sharply. "Your problem has always been that you play it safe. You think about every angle until the opportunity's gone." He gestured toward Jade. "A girl like this doesn't wait around for a man who plans his life on a spreadsheet."

Jade opened her mouth to speak, but Logan held up a hand. His voice, when it came, was calm and deliberate.

"Maybe I'm just done playing your game, Tyler."

Tyler scoffed, ready to land one final blow. "Playing it safe? Man, I tried to get you to go to Mexico after your dad... thought it would be good for you. You know what happened? Your mom called me. Told me to leave her son alone. That he wasn't ready. That you needed to stay put."

He shrugged. "Your whole life hasn't been careful, Lo. It's been curated."

The word hit like a punch.

Logan stared at him, stunned. "She what?"

"I'm serious. She said you'd been through enough. That you weren't meant for detours. That some journeys weren't for you."

Tyler's tone shifted—just a hair. A flicker of something dark and resentful surfaced in his eyes.

"Funny thing is, a week later, I ran into someone in Arizona. An older guy. Said he used to know your dad. Said he was chasing some map when he disappeared. Guy gave me this creepy little compass and said it wasn't finished yet." He gave a tight laugh. "I tossed it. Felt like bad luck."

Jade's blood ran cold. "What guy?"

Tyler shrugged. "I don't know. Weird eyes. Talked like he knew everything already. Said I wasn't the one he was waiting for." He narrowed his eyes at Jade. "Maybe he meant you."

She stared at him, too stunned to speak. Logan looked at her, then back at Tyler. The pieces weren't fitting yet—but they were tilting toward something.

Tyler gave a weak wave and disappeared into the crowd, swallowed by carnival lights and laughter.

They walked back to the Jeep in silence. The festive sounds of the fair felt jarring now, like a joke they didn't understand. The adrenaline from the confrontation drained away, leaving Logan reeling from a revelation that had just rewritten his entire life.

They reached the Jeep as the sun dipped below the rooftops, painting the sky in shades of orange and violet. In the relative peace of the empty parking lot, Logan's newfound steel had melted, replaced by a raw, shattered vulnerability.

He turned to her, his face a mask of confusion and pain. "Am I too careful?" he asked, his voice barely a whisper. "Is that why people leave?"

He wasn't just asking about Tyler. He was asking if anything he'd done had ever really been his choice—or if he'd just been moving through a script someone else had written.

And Jade, holding her father's broken compass in one hand and the memory of a stranger in Arizona in the other, had no idea how to answer.

But in her gut, she knew one thing: Tyler had given them more than a verbal punch. He'd just confirmed what she'd begun to fear.

They weren't the first people to follow this map.

And they weren't the only ones being watched.

Chapter 9: The Near-Fall

The question hung in the violet dusk between them, heavy and fragile.Am I too careful? Is that why people leave?

The vulnerability in Logan's voice was a raw, open wound, and Jade knew any answer she gave would be a weapon. A "no" would be a lie. A "yes" would be cruelty.

So she didn't answer with words.

She answered with action.

She reached into the Jeep, grabbed her father's map, and spread it across the hood. The paper felt electric under her fingertips.

"The clue says, 'At the heart of the falls, a new direction waits,'" she said, voice low but steady. She looked up, her eyes locking with his. "Let's go find it. Let's go be careless. Together."

It was a promise.

I'm not leaving.

Something shifted in Logan's expression. The confusion hardened into a raw, angry resolve. This was what he needed—not pity, but rebellion. Without another word, he got into the driver's seat. Jade slid in beside him.

The drive away from the fair was nothing like their previous journeys. He drove too fast. His hands were clenched on the wheel. The quiet, prepared teacher was gone—replaced by a man who had just watched the blueprint of his life catch fire.

"She called him," he said at last, voice taut with fury. "Tyler. My mother actually called him and told him to stay away. For my own good." His knuckles whitened. "What else has she done? What else has been 'curated'? My friends? My school? Did she decide who I got to be?"

He hit the steering wheel with the heel of his hand, a sharp, shocking burst of violence.

"Has my whole life been a choice—or just a collection of her fears?"

Jade just listened, the tension in the cab thick enough to drown in. Her own secrets felt smaller in the face of his unraveling—but no less heavy.

Because if Logan's mother had shaped his life from the shadows, who had been shaping hers?

They found the falls in a state park just as the last ranger was leaving for the night. It wasn't a gentle cascade. It was a roaring curtain of white water, crashing onto the rocks below with primal force. The air vibrated with it, a low thunder that rattled bones.

It felt like the edge of the world.

They searched the main overlook, finding nothing.

"The heart of the falls," Jade yelled over the roar. "It must be behind the water!"

Before Logan could protest, she climbed over the railing, landing on a wide, slick ledge of moss-covered stone that ran along the cliff face.

"Jade, wait!" Logan shouted, alarmed.

"I've got it!" she called back, edging closer to the pounding water, eyes scanning for a cave or carving.

The moss was slick under her boots. She took one more step—and the world tilted.

Her foot slipped. A strangled cry tore from her throat as her body pitched sideways into open air.

There was no time to think. Just the deafening roar and the moment of weightlessness before—

Impact. But not with the rocks below.

Logan.

He'd lunged. His arms locked around her waist like steel bands, carrying them both backward away from the edge. They crashed onto the solid path in a heap of tangled limbs, the force of it knocking the air from her lungs.

They lay there for a second, breathless, soaked in the cold mist. He was still holding her—tightly. Too tightly.

"What were you thinking?!" he roared, voice ragged with fear. He pushed himself up, hands on her shoulders, his face inches from hers. "You could have been killed! Don't you ever, ever do that again!"

It wasn't a command. It was a plea. A raw, panicked confession of terror.

But Jade, shaken, lashed out instead. "I had it under control!" she yelled, shoving at his chest. "Stop trying to manage me!"

"Manage you?!" he shouted, voice cracking. "I just found out my entire life has been a lie because my mother was too afraid of losing someone! And then I have to watch you almost throw yourself off a cliff?! I am not going to stand by and watch someone else I care about get hurt!"

The words echoed through the clearing.

Someone else I care about.

The fight went out of her instantly.

They were still kneeling on the path, breathless and soaked, the mist painting them in silver light.

She looked at his face—drawn, pale, terrified. There were a thousand things she could say. But she did the only one that felt true.

She surged forward and kissed him.

It wasn't gentle. It was desperate. Raw. Messy. It was everything they hadn't said and everything they were afraid to feel, all at once. His hands slid to her back, pulling her closer. Her fingers tangled in his damp shirt. They kissed like they'd been holding their breath for a week—and now could finally exhale.

When they finally broke apart, they were both trembling. The roar of the falls faded into the background, distant and irrelevant.

Then a sound cut through the moment.

A tinny ringtone, bright and insistent.

Logan's phone, left on the Jeep's dashboard, was ringing.

Still breathless, he stood and strode back to the Jeep, jaw set with new purpose. He snatched the phone from the dash.

"Mom," he said coldly. "We need to talk."

Jade could only hear his side of the conversation—short, clipped sentences.

"I know what you did... You had no right... I'm not a child... No, I'm not coming home."A long pause. "I have to go," he said, then hung up.

He stood still for a moment, his back to her. The air between them snapped taut.

Then he turned, face pale, eyes wide—not with relief.

With horror.

He held out the phone.

A new text had arrived. A screenshot of a map—their location—a bright blue dot blinking over the state park.

Beneath it, a message glowed.

I don't know who this girl is or what she's done to you, but I am coming to get my son.

Jade's heart stopped.

But it wasn't the message that chilled her.

It was the name of the file in the corner of the screenshot.

Watcher_Track_Active.jpg

Her pulse thudded in her ears.

She looked at Logan.

"They're not just tracking us," she whispered. "They're inside your phone."

His voice was quiet and horrified. "That's not my mother's tech."

They stared at each other, realization crashing down between them.

This wasn't just about overbearing parenting. Or a cold case. Or grief.

There was someone else.

Still out there.

Still watching.

And they'd just crossed a line they couldn't uncross.

Chapter 10: Breaking Point

He slowly turned around from the Jeep. The look on his face was not one of triumph. It was one of pure, dawning horror. For a split second, his eyes flickered to her lips, a silent, haunted acknowledgment of the kiss that had just changed everything, a connection now immediately tainted by crisis. Then he held out his phone for her to see.

The text message glowed in the twilight: *I am coming to get my son.*

The words hit Jade like a physical blow. Mrs. Hayes was right. Jade was the girl who had done this. She was the storm.

"We have to go," Logan said, his voice flat and panicked. "Now."

They scrambled back into the Jeep. The drive was a long, suffocating silence. He drove away from the falls, into the deepening night, with a hunted look in his eyes. Every pair of headlights in the rearview mirror was a potential threat.

Jade stared out the passenger window, caught in the gravity of her own worst fears. This is what she did. She pulled good, steady people into her orbit of chaos until they broke.

After an hour, Logan suddenly pulled the Jeep over onto a lonely, gravel shoulder on a dark stretch of road. He cut the engine. The sudden quiet was absolute.

He finally turned to her. "Say something," he pleaded, his voice ragged.

The dam inside her broke. "She's right," Jade whispered, her voice trembling. "This is my fault. This is what I *do*. I crash into people's lives, and I break things." Her voice cracked. "I did it to my best friend in college. I convinced him we were on some grand adventure, and he ended up... not okay. I don't get to make that mistake again. Not with you. You should go back to your safe harbor before I wreck your life for good."

He listened, his expression unreadable in the dark. But when he spoke, his voice was quiet, clear, and steady.

"Stop," he said.

She looked up, startled.

"Just... stop," he repeated, his gaze intense. "You didn't do this. I did this. For the first time in my life, Jade, I am making my own choice. I chose to get in this car. I chose to climb that hill. I chose to kiss you." He leaned forward, the space between them crackling. "This choice is *mine*. Don't you dare try to take it away from me by blaming yourself. Don't you dare make my first real choice about your regret."

He leaned closer, his voice dropping but gaining intensity. "You're not a storm, Jade. You're just the first person who was brave enough to knock on the door of a house I didn't even realize was a prison. Don't be sorry you knocked. I'm not."

His words were a stunning, radical act of ownership, a validation that stole her breath. He wasn't just claiming his choices; he was rewriting her very identity, turning her greatest fear about herself into a strength.

With a newfound resolve, Logan reached into the glove compartment, took out his phone, and held the power button down. The screen glowed, then went black. He had severed the tracker. He had cut the final cord. The silence that followed was different. It wasn't tense or awkward. It was the clean, quiet, terrifying silence of true, untethered freedom.

He looked at her, his face illuminated only by the faint, distant starlight. "Okay," he said, his voice perfectly steady. "The map. Where to next?"

Jade didn't answer right away. She simply reached over, took the map from the seat between them, and spread it across the dashboard. The faint starlight illuminated the cryptic lines her father had drawn. Then, she took out the tarnished, broken compass and placed it deliberately in the very center of the map.

It was an offering. An acceptance. A new starting point.

Chapter 11: Crossroads

The drive to the campground was a long, quiet hum of engine and asphalt. The furious energy of their flight had given way to a shared, bone-deep exhaustion. Neither of them spoke, but the silence wasn't entirely empty. It was taut, frayed at the edges with everything left unsaid.

They finally found Coyote Run after midnight, a deserted patch of land tucked beneath a sky so vast and full of stars it felt like they'd driven to the top of the world. The air was too still. The isolation should have been a comfort. Instead, it felt like an accusation.

Logan pitched a small, two-person tent with practiced efficiency, his movements automatic. Then he went back to the Jeep and pulled out a second, identical tent bag. He stood holding it for a long moment, just staring. When he looked at Jade, his eyes held a silent question—a vulnerability so unguarded it nearly buckled her.

She looked away first. "I can set that one up," she said quietly, nodding at the spare tent. Her voice felt hollow. The look of faint, resigned disappointment that passed across his face hit harder than anything he'd said.

They sat near the crackling campfire afterward, nursing whiskey in silence. The bottle passed between them like a peace offering neither knew how to accept.

"I keep replaying it," Logan said finally, eyes fixed on the flames. "The phone call. The map. Tyler. It's like finding out the book you've been reading your whole life has pages missing. Pages someone else tore out."

Jade didn't answer right away. Her hands were curled around the silver flask, fingers tight, knuckles pale. Wanting to meet his vulnerability with something real, she reached for her wallet and pulled out a few worn slips of paper, folded into tiny squares.

"I have… a thing," she said. "For my mistakes. My Regret Jar. A way of owning them so they don't own me."

He glanced over, curiosity tempered by caution. "Can I see one?"

She passed him one, heart thudding. He unfolded it slowly and read:

Let someone get too close on a road trip. Panicked and ran. Lost him forever.

His face changed—not with judgment, but with something else. Recognition. He carefully folded the slip and handed it back to her.

"My jar would be full of all the things I didn't do," he said, voice barely audible above the fire's crackle. "All the trips not taken. All the words not said. My dad... he wasn't perfect, but I never told him I was proud of him. Never told him anything, really."

"Maybe we're both just trying to figure out how to live with our ghosts," she said, more to the flames than to him.

A breeze stirred through the campsite, carrying with it a strange sound—a faint rustle behind the treeline. Too deliberate to be wind. Logan stiffened. His hand brushed against the flashlight beside him, fingers tensing.

Jade stood slowly, heart racing. "Probably just an animal."

They both turned as a soft metallic clink echoed in the dark.

"Did you hear that?" Logan asked.

"Yeah," she whispered.

He grabbed the flashlight and swept it across the trees. Nothing. Just the hollow silhouettes of gnarled trunks and the flicker of moths in the beam.

"I'm going to turn in," he said at last, voice flat. He retreated to his tent, zipping the flap shut with a slow finality.

Jade stayed by the fire. Another twig snapped in the darkness—closer this time. She froze. Her ears strained against the silence, her pulse roaring. A beat passed. Then another. Nothing.

She forced herself to breathe.

It's just nerves. Stress. That's all.

But when she finally stood to douse the fire, her eyes landed on something resting where she had been sitting minutes earlier.

The heart-shaped stone from Storm King's Peak.

Her blood ran cold.

And resting on top of it was a small, folded piece of paper, so white it nearly glowed in the dying coals' light.

She picked it up with trembling fingers. The handwriting was neat, unfamiliar, blocky.

THE TREASURE IS NOT WHAT YOU THINK.

A chill raced down her spine.

Someone had been here. Not earlier. Not days ago.

Tonight.

They'd left a message.

And they were watching.

Chapter 12: Sylvie's Wisdom

THE TREASURE IS NOT WHAT YOU THINK .The words were still etched into Jade's skull when she jolted Logan awake, her voice a breathless whisper laced with panic.

"Logan. Wake up. Someone was here."

He was already grabbing the flashlight, eyes narrowing as she thrust the stone and note into his hands. His gaze skimmed the message, then flicked to the familiar heart-shaped stone from Storm King's Peak. The combination made him go very still.

"This was on your log?"

Jade nodded. "It wasn't there when I stood up. Someone placed it while I was walking the perimeter."

They swept the campsite in tense silence, beams of light slicing through the pre-dawn dark. But the forest held its secrets. No footprints. No broken twigs. No noise but the wind in the trees.

That was somehow worse.

"We need to move," Jade said, voice clipped. "Now."

They packed with brutal efficiency, paranoia stinging every motion. As the Jeep roared down the highway under a bruised morning sky, Jade caught herself checking the rearview mirror every few seconds. But there was nothing. Just a rising, invisible pressure she couldn't shake.

They reached The Crystal Caverns just after dawn. The tourist center was still dark, but nestled in the rear gravel lot sat a brightly painted Airstream trailer. Smoke curled from a chimney, scented with cedar and sage.

Before they could knock, the door opened.

A woman stepped out holding a mug of tea. She was lean, late forties maybe, with a silver braid and dark eyes that scanned like floodlights. She took one look at them and tilted her head.

"You're early," she said, voice rough and warm. "Or very, very late. You two have the look."

Jade didn't even bother with a smile. "We're following a map."

The woman's eyes flicked to the tarnished token Jade pulled from her pocket. She studied it for a beat longer than necessary, then nodded. "Come on. Name's Sylvie."

She led them around back to a rock garden where dozens of painted river stones were nestled in tall cairns. "The toll isn't money," she explained, handing them each a flat stone and a brush. "You don't get to move forward until you leave something behind."

They crouched on the ground in silence. Jade painted a shattered jar spilling slips of paper. On the other side, a key. Her fingers shook the entire time.

Logan painted a bird in a cage. Then a winding open road.

When they finished, Sylvie studied the stones in silence.

"Pretty hard to walk a road when the cage is bolted from the inside," she said to Logan. Then she turned to Jade. "And keys only matter if you know what you're unlocking. Or who."

Jade stiffened. "What does that mean?"

Sylvie didn't answer. She just motioned toward the Airstream. "Wait here."

She returned with a weathered composition notebook and handed it to Jade. "Your father left this with me a long time ago. Said if someone with your eyes ever showed up, I'd know who to give it to."

Jade's hands were numb. The handwriting on the first page punched the air from her lungs.

"For Jade. If you've come this far, then it means I never finished what I started. I'm sorry."

The pages inside were disjointed—sketches of landmarks, frantic scrawls about energy fields, directional markers, astronomical alignments. And then:

A hand-drawn feather. Black. Ragged.Beneath it: THE WATCHER COMES FOR THE LOST. SHE NEVER STOPS.

Jade stared at the ink. Her mind reeled.

"I saw that feather," she whispered. "Twice. On the Jeep dashboard, and once at the campsite."

Sylvie lowered herself to sit beside them. "He was terrified near the end," she said. "Not of dying. Of being followed. He talked about a woman who wasn't really a woman. Who didn't age. He called her the Watcher."

Jade looked up sharply. "Like a ghost?"

Sylvie shook her head. "Worse. Something intentional. Something that follows broken people who chase meaning too hard. He said she didn't care about gold or treasure. She just wanted to be the one at the end of every story."

Logan paled. "So she followed him."

"Maybe," Sylvie said. "Or maybe he summoned her without meaning to. Some people chase ghosts so long they attract them."

She stood, brushed off her pants. "You said the next clue was at the heart of the falls. Did you find it?"

Jade hesitated. "Yes. But no marker. Just the waterfall. And the note. And this."

She reached into her pocket and handed Sylvie the heart-shaped stone and the second note.

Sylvie read the message. Her brows knit.

THE TREASURE IS NOT WHAT YOU THINK. HE WAS MINE FIRST.

Sylvie exhaled through her nose. "Then she's real. And she's not just watching."

Jade's fingers twitched around the edges of the notebook. "So what does she want?"

Sylvie looked between them. "Legacy. Devotion. Control. Maybe all of it. Some people can't bear to be forgotten, Jade. They'd rather haunt the living than be lost to the past."

Logan rubbed a hand down his face. "And now she's following us."

"Not following," Sylvie corrected. "Directing."

She pointed toward the rear of the Airstream where a small tourist map of the region was pinned to a bulletin board. A red circle was marked in the lower right corner.

"Your father planned to head here next. Ember Cliffs. Said it was where 'fire meets sky.' You can go. But if you do, you need to know this: she won't stop now. Not until you confront what he never did."

Jade moved to the map, traced the route with her fingertip. The land out there was remote. Stark. Perfect for getting lost—or for someone else to get close without being seen.

As Logan packed up their gear, Jade remained behind for a moment. She glanced again at the painted stones in the garden. One sat apart from the rest—black feather painted on one side, a face sketched on the other.

The face was half-finished.

The eyes... looked like hers.

She stared at it for a long time, stomach churning.

When she finally got in the Jeep, Logan handed her the torn, battered tourist map they'd marked up. "Backup plan," he said. "Since the real one's gone."

Jade nodded and tried to smile.

But the Watcher had already rewritten the route.

And now, they were following her.

Chapter 13: Lost Without a Map

The feather lay on the dashboard, gleaming black against the pale vinyl. Beside it sat the rusted safety pin—small, innocuous, and absolutely chilling.

Jade's hands trembled as she picked it up. The weight of it wasn't physical. It was something older. Sharper.

"I haven't seen this since I was a kid," she whispered. "My dad always kept one like this on his pack. Said it was for emergencies. A dumb superstition."

Logan was silent beside her, jaw clenched. "It's not dumb if someone left it to rattle you."

She turned it over in her fingers. "But how would they know? About the pin. About the map. About any of this?"

"They've been following us," he said grimly. "Watching us. Listening, maybe. Long enough to know what matters."

She didn't respond. The dread had crystallized. This wasn't just about clues and riddles. Someone was inside this journey with them—rewriting it in real time.

And now the map was gone.

"We have to go inside," Logan said suddenly, with a kind of tight urgency. "Whoever they are... they've already seen everything. We need to stay one step ahead."

Jade wasn't sure what terrified her more—the thief or the idea that they might already be too late. Still, she followed him into the cavern's gaping mouth.

The air was cooler inside, damp and laced with the metallic scent of minerals and time. Their footsteps echoed unnaturally, muffled by the porous stone. It wasn't claustrophobic, not exactly. But it felt like the earth was listening.

At the first fork, they split without speaking. Logan veered left. Jade went right, instinct pulling her toward the sound of water.

The deeper she went, the more surreal it became—veins of quartz glowing faintly beneath the rock, forming patterns she couldn't tell were natural or designed. The hair on her arms stood on end.

Finally, she found it.

A narrow waterfall, half-hidden behind a curtain of glittering stone, trickled down a rock face into a crystal-clear pool. It shimmered with light from some unknown source, glowing faintly like something alive.

She should've felt victorious. Instead, she felt... hollow.

A victory without a map didn't feel like a win. It felt like drifting.

She turned to go—and saw movement.

A flashlight beam cutting across a distant tunnel.

"Logan?" she called softly.

No answer.

The light vanished.

Her breath caught in her throat.

She stepped quickly away from the pool and back into the corridor, retracing her steps with careful haste.

Then, a soft scrape behind her.

She whipped around.

No one.

No light. No voice.

Just the rush of blood in her ears and the slow drip of mineral water onto stone.

She turned back—and nearly collided with Logan as he rounded the corner, flashlight high.

"You okay?" he asked, voice sharp.

"I thought I saw…" Her voice faltered. "I'm not sure."

He scanned the tunnel behind her. "You found it?"

She nodded. "The waterfall. But no clue. No marker. Just water and stone."

They stood in the flickering silence. Logan finally broke it. "We need a new plan."

Outside, the sun was fully up. Sylvie was waiting beside the Airstream, arms folded, gaze unreadable. When she saw their faces, she didn't speak—just gestured them inside.

They sat across from her at a small table inside the trailer, the smell of lavender and cedar thick in the air.

Sylvie poured tea with practiced ease. "I take it you've lost more than your direction."

Jade exhaled shakily. "Someone's following us. They've taken the map. They've been… leaving things. Feathers. Notes. A pin from my dad's old hiking pack."

Sylvie didn't flinch. "Did you tell anyone you were coming here?"

Jade shook her head. "Not really. Just Ruby. And even she didn't know the whole route."

Sylvie nodded slowly. "Then someone knew before you did. Or they were waiting for someone to follow the map again."

Logan leaned forward. "Again?"

Sylvie's eyes drifted toward the window. "Years ago, a man came through here with a similar map. Said he was chasing a legend. Had this wild idea that there was something buried beneath the caverns—something his daughter was supposed to find someday."

Jade's throat closed. "That was my father."

Sylvie's gaze sharpened. "Then this journey didn't start with you. And it's not just about treasure. It's about legacy. Regret. Obsession." She reached under the table and pulled out a battered composition notebook. "He left this with me. Said if anyone ever came through with that same haunted look in their eyes, I'd know who to give it to."

Jade took the notebook like it might combust. Her father's handwriting sprawled across the first page: "For Jade. If you ever come this far, you deserve the truth."

She opened it slowly, heart in her throat.

Inside were pages of erratic notes, sketches of landmarks, theories, cryptic symbols. And near the end—a drawing of the feather. A black feather, scratched in furious ink strokes, with one word beneath it.

Watcher.

Jade stared at it.

She felt it again—the subtle chill on the back of her neck.

They weren't just being followed.

They were being tracked.

Sylvie stood and crossed to a small drawer. She returned with a folded tourist map of the surrounding region and spread it on the table. "You need to keep moving. If the original map's gone, you'll have to rely on memory, instinct, and whatever your father left behind."

Logan nodded slowly. "We think the next clue involved 'the place where fire meets sky.' He said something like that in the notebook."

Sylvie tapped a red marker on the map. "Could be Ember Cliffs. Out past the ravine. Desert country."

As Logan traced the route, Jade noticed something on the side of the map. A dark smudge in the margin. She leaned closer.

It was a fingerprint.

Fresh.

Her skin crawled.

They hadn't just taken the map. They had touched everything.

Even this.

She looked at Logan. "We need to go. Now."

Outside, the sun blazed too bright in the empty sky. The world felt too open. Too exposed.

They got in the Jeep without another word. As Logan started the engine, Jade glanced back one last time at the Airstream. Sylvie stood in the doorway, her silhouette framed in the rising light.

"Be careful who you follow," she called softly.

They didn't ask what she meant.

They just drove.

As the dust kicked up behind them and the last hint of civilization fell away, Jade reached into her jacket pocket, fingers brushing over the safety pin. It felt heavier now. Not like a relic.

Like a warning.

And in her mind, one phrase echoed with a clarity that made her blood run cold:

The treasure is not what you think.

Chapter 14: The Whispering Wall

They left Sylvie's trailer in silence, the early afternoon sun casting long, surreal shadows through the dusty pine. The Jeep's tires crunched over gravel as Logan turned onto the unpaved back road toward Ember Cliffs.

Jade held her father's notebook in her lap, fingers brushing over the warning again.

THE WATCHER COMES FOR THE LOST. SHE NEVER STOPS.

The words felt heavier than ink. Like they'd been etched in something older than fear.

She traced the feather sketch again—black, jagged, off-center. The same one that had appeared twice before. Only now she wondered if it hadn't been left...

...but returned.

"She marked him," Jade said aloud, not realizing she'd spoken until Logan glanced over.

"What?"

She met his eyes. "My father. That stone—the one with the feather. It wasn't just a symbol. It was a marker. Like a claim."

Logan's jaw tightened. "So now she's claiming you too."

The words hit like a slap. She didn't respond.

They drove for hours. The landscape changed—sharper hills, scrubby redbrush, the scent of scorched earth rising as they approached Ember Cliffs. It was more than a name. The soil was literally scorched in places, dark ash curling in the wind. No signs. No trail markers. Just a jagged canyon and a half-collapsed fence around a chain-locked iron gate.

Jade hopped out, map in one hand, notebook in the other. Logan tried the gate—locked, rusted.

She crouched, checking the corner post. A strip of bark had been peeled away to reveal faint symbols beneath.

"It's a cipher," she murmured. "Same style as the carvings at the first overlook."

Logan scanned the canyon below. "This was a mining site. Abandoned after a fire."

She turned the page in the notebook.

Cliff's edge. West of the whispering wall. Listen for the breath between.She hates silence.

"That doesn't sound ominous at all," Logan muttered.

They climbed a goat trail around the fence and followed the edge of the ravine, the sun angling low in the sky behind them. Wind scraped across the rocks, whistling through the scorched brush.

Then they heard it.

Whispers.

Faint. Barely there. But not wind.

Language? No. Murmurs. Like thoughts you couldn't quite catch.

Jade's spine went rigid. "There."

A wide basalt slab jutted from the cliffside. At first glance, it looked like just another rock face—until you got close. Then you saw the etchings.

Dozens of them. Hundreds. Names. Symbols. Fractured phrases etched in dozens of hands.

Where is she?I told her the truthShe took him anywayNo more echoes. No more silence.

Jade stepped closer and pressed her hand to the surface. It was cold. Colder than the wind. Colder than it should've been in the blazing heat.

Then she heard it—clearer.

Not a whisper.

A word.

"Run."

She jerked back. "Did you hear that?"

Logan was staring at the wall, eyes wide. "Yeah."

They both turned at the same time.

A single feather. Black, curled at the tip, lay at their feet.

"I didn't see it fall," Logan said, voice hollow. "It wasn't there a second ago."

Jade knelt slowly and picked it up.

Beneath it, pressed into the ash: a single print. A boot tread.

Small.

Female.

But the pattern was old-fashioned. Like something from another era.

Jade's voice shook. "There's no one else here."

She flipped the notebook to the last page. It was blank—except for a smear of ink where something had once been written, then wiped away. A shadow of letters remained.

She tilted the page into the light.

...watching me... not alone... the girl... hers now...

The words made her nauseous.

They weren't her father's handwriting.

"Let's go," she said, voice brittle. "Let's get back to the Jeep."

But when they returned to the ridge...

The Jeep was gone.

Logan's voice broke the silence. "I parked it right here."

Jade's pulse spiked. "It's not possible—"

Then they saw it.

Sitting on the flat rock where the Jeep had been.

A Polaroid photograph.

Jade stepped forward and picked it up. Her breath caught.

It was a photo of her—taken at Storm King's Peak. Not during the hike. After. When she'd stood alone at the overlook, arms crossed, staring into the fog.

A time when no one had been with her.

A time she thought she'd been alone.

Scrawled in jagged black marker on the back of the photo:

"Every story has a thief. This one was never yours."

She turned to Logan. "She's not just following us anymore."

He nodded grimly.

"She's leading."

Chapter 15: The Echo Path

Not just moved. Not vandalized.

Gone.

Jade turned in a slow, disbelieving circle, her boots grinding ash into the parched earth. The empty stretch of red dust and low brush offered no tracks, no trail, not even the sound of an engine fading into the distance.

"This can't be real," Logan said, his voice strangled. "It was here. Right here. Keys in my pocket."

He pulled them out and shook them as if expecting the vehicle to reappear like a magic trick. They clinked dully in his palm.

Jade gripped the Polaroid tighter. The image was just beginning to curl at the edges. She could see the faint outline of herself — head tilted at the overlook, the sky behind her bleached and cloudless.

No one else had been there.

Except, clearly, someone had.

"She's changing the route," Jade whispered.

Logan turned sharply. "What?"

"She's controlling the story. That's what Sylvie said. 'Not following—directing.' We thought we were chasing answers, but we've been walking her path the whole time."

He opened his mouth, but there was no argument. Only a shared recognition, heavy and inevitable.

"We need to move," Jade said. "If we stay here, we're sitting ducks."

"To where?" Logan asked, sweeping the barren horizon. "We're twenty miles from the nearest town. No cell reception. No water. No Jeep."

Jade exhaled slowly and reached into her backpack. She pulled out her father's notebook and the marked tourist map Sylvie had given them. The pages fluttered in the hot wind.

"She circled an alternate site," Jade murmured. "The Echo Path. It's less than four miles west."

Logan looked skeptical. "And what exactly is the Echo Path?"

Jade hesitated. "She didn't say. Just that it was the place he stopped trusting himself."

They started walking.

The cliffs loomed to their right, the sky darkening as the heat of the day bled into a restless twilight. The silence was thick—oppressive. Even the insects seemed muted here.

An hour in, they passed a rock formation shaped like a broken lyre. Etched into the base were five words:

"You only hear what echoes."

Logan trailed his hand across the grooves. "What does that even mean?"

Jade wasn't sure.

They kept moving.

Half an hour later, the path narrowed between two vertical stone walls that curved inward like open jaws. The temperature dropped ten degrees as they entered. The hair on Jade's arms stood up.

Whispers began.

At first it was like wind skimming stone.

Then it became voices.

Their voices.

"Is that why people leave?""I don't run—I just don't wait.""She's mine now."

Jade's breath caught. "That's... us."

"From earlier," Logan said, pale. "That's exactly what we said."

She turned in a full circle, trying to find a speaker, a trick. But there was nothing.

Only stone.

Only echoes.

Then another voice cut through. Not theirs.

Low. Female. Smooth as silk dragged across bone.

"You were never the hero.You were just the map."

Jade froze.

"What did it say?" Logan asked.

But she couldn't speak. Her throat had closed around it.

They reached a widening in the path where someone had built a crude altar from stacked bones and burnt wood. A tin photo frame sat at the top. Inside: an image of her father. But his face had been scratched out.

Carved below it:

"What she gives, she owns."

Jade stepped back. Her pulse thundered.

"Logan," she said quietly, "I don't think she's just watching us."

He turned. "What do you mean?"

"I think she's rewriting who we are."

Wind gusted through the canyon, and a torn scrap of paper fluttered out from the altar's base. Jade caught it as it blew past. It was old, weather-worn.

A single sentence scrawled across the center in blood-brown ink:

"You don't leave the story. You become it."

Suddenly, everything shifted. The stone around them rippled—just slightly, as if breathing. A high-pitched ringing began to echo from deep inside the canyon.

Jade grabbed Logan's arm. "We have to go."

They turned and ran, the canyon seemingly tightening behind them. Voices followed—first whispers, then laughter, then screams that never broke into sound. Just vibrations, like pain converted into frequency.

They burst from the pass just as the sun dipped below the cliffs. The air hit them like a slap—hot, dry, real.

Silence returned.

The whispering stopped.

So did the ringing.

They collapsed beside a boulder, lungs heaving.

After a long moment, Logan turned to her, sweat streaking his face.

"This isn't just about your dad, is it?"

Jade shook her head. "No. It's bigger."

She pulled the photo frame from her pack, looked at the scratched-out face. "He tried to warn me. He said she wasn't a ghost. She was a presence. A need. A hunger."

Logan's voice was hoarse. "What does she want?"

Jade thought about it.

Control.

Devotion.

Legacy.

She looked down at the paper in her hand again.

"You don't leave the story. You become it."

"She wants to be the author," Jade said. "Of everything."

Logan frowned. "And us?"

"She wants to write us in... and then erase us."

They stared into the rising night.

Far in the distance, a light flickered.

Not a star.

Not a fire.

It pulsed once.

Then again.

A signal.

And somehow... they both knew.

It was for them.

Chapter 16: The Signal Below

They followed the flickering light through a burned ravine that smelled of scorched pine and dry stone. No stars above—just a sickle moon, the sky smeared with cloud like smudged ink. Every step felt like stepping deeper into a story someone else was writing in real time.

Jade clutched the paper from the altar—You don't leave the story. You become it. It had become more than a warning. It felt like a contract.

The light moved slowly across the dark valley, pulsing in a pattern—two short, one long. Then pause. Then again.

Logan angled his head. "It's not fire. Could be an LED. Low wattage. Portable."

"Or a trap," Jade said.

He didn't disagree.

They reached a ridge overlooking a canyon hollowed into the land like a forgotten wound. At the bottom: an old mining outpost. Rusted corrugated roofs sagged inward. A tangle of steel cables lay like discarded webbing. One building—smaller, almost shacklike—emitted the flickering light from its open window.

Logan pulled out binoculars. "No movement. No heat signature. But... something's reflecting in there. Metal or glass, maybe."

Jade stared at the shack. Her skin buzzed.

"Wait," she said. "There."

A figure.

Not walking—gliding.

Female silhouette. Long dark dress. Unmoving arms.

Then it vanished behind the shack.

Logan lowered the binoculars slowly. "Did you see—"

"I saw."

They descended in silence, the crunch of gravel underfoot unnaturally loud. The buildings loomed like decaying teeth, their shadows alive with wind and memory.

The door to the shack was ajar.

Inside, a single oil lamp flickered on a rickety table. Beneath it, a journal. And beside that...

A cassette recorder.

Jade stared at it. "My dad used to have one of these. He used it when he didn't trust digital files."

She pressed play.

Static hissed. Then a voice—quiet, low, brittle.

Her father's.

"She's in the seams. Not a person. A pattern. She becomes what you fear. Or what you need. She writes herself into absence. Into loss. Into legacy."

A pause. Then a cough. Then:

"If Jade finds this... I'm sorry. I tried to bury her. But I couldn't stop digging. And she... she waited."

Logan moved to the journal. He flipped through it, brows furrowed. "Schematics. Pressure systems. Coordinates. She told him where to go."

"She guided him," Jade whispered. "Just like she's doing to us."

She reached into the notebook's back flap and pulled out a folded page.

It was a map.

Drawn by hand. But not her father's.

Too elegant.

Too precise.

Across the bottom in that same inhumanly neat script:

"The End is a Beginning. But only for One."

Behind them, something creaked.

Jade turned.

The woman was standing outside the doorway. Still. Too still.

No eyes visible beneath the brim of a wide black hat. No breath.

Just presence.

Then—

She lifted one hand.

Held up a feather.

Let it fall.

It didn't drift.

It dropped like a stone.

Logan slammed the door shut.

They bolted the rear exit and scrambled out through a collapsed back wall, sprinting toward a narrow tunnel that opened beside a rusted minecart track. They ducked inside just as the shack exploded behind them—not with fire, but with silence. Deafening, crushing silence. As if sound had been deleted.

They kept running, breath ragged, the tunnel growing colder.

Finally, the passage opened into a chamber of shattered rock and old mining equipment. In the center stood a circular hatch set into the floor—sealed tight.

Jade reached for the release lever. It didn't budge.

Logan pointed. "Wait—on the wall."

Carved into the stone:

"The one who opens the door must forget the way back."

Jade's breath caught. "What does that mean?"

Logan looked at her. "It means if we go through... we might not remember how we got here."

She hesitated.

Then: "We're already in the story. If we stop now, we just become a footnote."

Together, they pulled the lever.

The hatch creaked, then slowly opened.

A ladder descended into darkness.

Jade looked back—once.

The woman was standing at the tunnel mouth.

Still watching.

Still waiting.

Jade swallowed hard, then descended.

Logan followed.

The hatch sealed above them.

And the story continued.

Chapter 17: The Archive of the Unwritten

The ladder descended farther than it should have. Too far. Minutes passed in silence, the metal rungs slick with condensation, the walls narrowing, the air thinning with a faint, metallic bite.

Jade stopped counting after the hundredth rung.

Finally, her boots touched solid ground.

A narrow corridor stretched out before her, carved not by machinery but by design. Etchings lined the walls—symbols she didn't recognize but instinctively understood. They pulsed faintly, like veins carrying breath instead of blood.

Logan landed beside her with a grunt, the hatch above sealing shut.

"This place isn't on any map," he said.

"It's beneath one," she replied.

They moved forward, each footstep swallowed by the silence. There was no ambient hum, no echo. Just stillness. The kind that felt... expectant.

Then the hall opened into a chamber unlike anything they'd seen.

A circular space—walls lined with scrolls, books, film reels, tablets, all arranged by shape, not age or language. Each object sat within a recessed alcove, bathed in a soft amber glow.

At the center stood a dais. Upon it: a pedestal with a blank, leather-bound book.

Not untouched.

Waiting.

Jade approached. The book pulsed faintly beneath her fingers.

Logan spoke softly. "This isn't just an archive."

"No," she whispered. "It's a memory vault."

"But none of this is recorded history. Look—"

He lifted a scroll. The script shifted as he tilted it. From cursive to block print to runes.

"These aren't stories that were written," he said, awed. "They're stories that were almost written."

"Unmade decisions," Jade said.

"Unlived lives."

She opened the leather-bound book on the pedestal.

Its pages were blank—until she touched one.

Then ink bloomed across it.

Jade Sinclair descended into the Archive knowing the cost of remembering might be the loss of herself. The Watcher was close now. Close enough to turn breath into script.

She recoiled. "It's writing itself."

"No," Logan said, staring at the page. "It's writing you."

Footsteps echoed behind them.

They turned.

Nothing.

Then:

A soft flutter. Black feathers scattered on the floor behind them—no bird, no wind, just the aftermath of something unseen.

A door appeared in the wall.

It hadn't been there before.

Jade approached cautiously. The moment she laid her hand on the frame, the leather-bound book slammed shut. The glow in the chamber dimmed.

The door opened inward, revealing a room of mirrors.

No walls—just reflections.

Endless versions of Jade. Some older, some broken, some with eyes like empty wells. One was smiling. But not kindly.

Each reflection moved independently.

Each held a book.

Each book had a different title.

The Girl Who DisappearedThe Watcher's DaughterThe Feathered LieAuthor: Jade Sinclair

Jade stepped back.

"What is this?" she breathed.

Logan pointed toward the farthest mirror. "That one. Look."

A version of Jade—scarred, hunched, hollow—was writing in her book. As her pen moved, pain rippled across the other reflections. Some shattered. One bled.

And on her page:

To become the author, she must erase the reader.

Jade backed out of the mirror chamber, heart hammering.

She faced Logan. "This is what my father saw. This is what broke him."

He nodded grimly. "The Watcher doesn't just want to be part of the story. She wants to be the only one left in it."

Suddenly the ground rumbled. Lights in the alcoves began to flicker.

"She knows we're here," Logan said.

The pedestal book cracked open again. A new sentence appeared:

One must choose to forget. The other must choose to stay.

Jade's hands trembled. "It's giving us a choice."

"No," Logan said. "It's giving us a role."

A feather drifted down from nowhere.

On the back of it, written in the same elegant script:

"The End is a Beginning. But only for One."

They stared at the message.

"I'm not letting you stay behind," Logan said.

"And I'm not letting you forget."

For a moment, neither moved.

Then Jade looked at the leather-bound book, the mirror chamber, the archive walls pulsing with possible lives. Her father's voice echoed in her memory.

She becomes what you fear. Or what you need.

"What if she's not just following us?" Jade said. "What if she is us—in versions we never chose to be?"

Logan exhaled slowly. "Then she's already inside us."

The rumble grew louder.

The pedestal book flipped to its final page.

A blank line.

Waiting for a name.

Jade stepped forward.

And wrote:

Jade Sinclair remembers. And rewrites.

The chamber shuddered.

The mirrors cracked.

The walls bled light.

And the book burst into flame.

Chapter 18: The Rewrite

They woke in the dust.

Jade opened her eyes to gray light filtering through dead branches. The Archive was gone. No hatch. No chamber. Just cracked desert earth and the distant screech of wind.

Beside her, Logan stirred. "Are we...?"

"I don't know," she whispered. "But we're not where we were."

The world looked the same—sort of.

Except for the sky.

It was wrong.

Familiar stars rearranged into new constellations. Orion missing. The Big Dipper crooked. The air shimmered, not from heat but from static—like memory erasing itself in slow motion.

She sat up.

Her backpack was still with her. Inside: the map. But it was blank now. The trail gone. The towns missing.

Only one word had been written across the middle: THE END.

Logan leaned on his elbow. "Where's the Archive?"

Jade didn't answer right away. She reached into her pocket, half afraid of what she might find.

The feather was still there.

Only now, it was blackened—charred at the edges, curling inward.

"She didn't disappear," Jade said quietly. "She adapted."

A crack split the ground nearby—just a foot long, an inch wide, but deep. Too deep.

Like a paper tear through the world.

They stood.

In the far distance, a town flickered into view.

It blinked once—on, then off—like a projection losing power.

"Logan," she said, pointing. "Look."

As they stared, the landscape between them and the town began to shimmer. The terrain reshaped, subtly at first—rock formations twisting, shadows elongating, brush shifting positions as if the script beneath the land was being retyped in real time.

"She's rewriting the world," Logan whispered.

"No," Jade said. "She's rewriting me."

The sound came then.

A low, rhythmic clicking—like a typewriter in the dark.

They turned.

The Watcher was standing fifty feet away, still as a statue. Her face was visible now. It wasn't monstrous. It was p erfect.Too perfect. Every feature symmetrical. Eyes empty but aware.

She raised one hand.

A page floated down between them.

Jade caught it midair.

On it:

"Let go. Become the ending."

Jade's hands trembled. The paper felt real. But the words throbbed, like they could crawl.

She crushed it in her fist.

"No," she said. "You don't get to finish my story."

The Watcher didn't flinch. But the world around them did.

Sky fractured. Earth cracked. The town ahead pixelated, then vanished entirely.

Logan grabbed her wrist. "We have to run."

"No," Jade said. "Running is her ending."

She pulled out her father's notebook. Flipped to the back.

There—beneath layers of notes and codes—was a phrase she hadn't seen before. Written in faint pencil:

"The thread breaks where the truth begins."

Jade looked up. "There's a place he didn't want anyone to find. Not even me."

She turned to Logan. "It's the origin point. Where he first met her. Where she took shape. If we find it—if we cut the thread—maybe we stop her."

"How do we find it?" he asked.

She looked out over the fractured land. "We don't follow the story anymore. We unwrite it."

Jade pulled out a pen. Found the back of the now-blank map.

And wrote:

"She never reached the origin."

The moment the ink dried, the land ahead shifted.

The flickering town disappeared.

Replaced by something else.

A single tree. Atop a red hill. A gash in the ground before it, glowing softly with violet light.

A memory scar.

"I think that's it," Jade said.

They walked toward it, the world rippling around them with every step. Behind them, the Watcher followed—but slower now. Like she was losing ground.

Or losing control.

They reached the tree as the wind picked up.

Below it, a stone marker. Unreadable at first, until Jade brushed away the dust.

Here lies the last author.May her story rest.

Jade touched the stone.

And suddenly—

She remembered.

The cabin. The journals. Her father whispering at night to a blank page, then tearing it out before it could write itself.

The first time she found a feather in her crib.

The way her mother left without a trace.

It was never just paranoia.

It was protection.

"Logan," she said, shaking. "She's not just a presence. She's a parasite."

He nodded slowly. "Feeding on authors. On their possibility."

Jade stood. "Then I'm going to starve her."

She pulled out the map one last time.

And wrote:

"She ended before she began."

The ground shuddered.

The Watcher screamed—a soundless, terrible howl as her outline fragmented. She reached for them. But her hands blurred, dissolved into ash mid-motion.

The typewriter sound stopped.

The wind stopped.

And then—

Everything went still.

Chapter 19: The First Line

They didn't move at first.

Jade stood beneath the tree, breath shallow, the last of the Watcher's ash curling skyward like smoke from a forgotten fire.

The air felt... weightless. Like it had been rewritten, too.

Logan's hand found hers—firm, grounding. "Are you still with me?"

She looked down at their intertwined fingers, then up at him. "I think I am."

And she was. Not just present, but *whole.* She could feel herself again. Not scattered across possible versions. Not slipping into someone else's sentence.

Just Jade.

Jade Sinclair.

She let out a slow breath. "It's over."

"For now," Logan said. "She's part of the story. But so are we."

They turned to leave—but paused.

The red hill behind them remained. The gravestone of the last author stood silent.

The wind carried no words anymore.

Only memory.

The return hike was slow.

The land no longer shifted beneath their steps. No flickering towns. No impossible paths. Just earth. Rock. Sky. Familiar, and imperfect.

By dusk, they reached the rusted Jeep, parked exactly where they'd left it—except the Polaroid was gone.

In its place, on the dashboard, sat the blackened feather.

And beneath it, a single sheet of paper. Typewritten.

Jade picked it up, heart racing.

You rewrote me. But the story remembers.Be careful what you author next.

She folded it carefully, placed it in her pocket without a word.

Logan didn't ask. He just opened the passenger door.

They checked into a roadside motel outside Flagstaff.

Jade stepped out of the shower and found Logan sitting on the floor beside the bed, the map spread out in front of him. It was blank again, but this time not eerie—just waiting.

Like paper always does.

He looked up. "What if we didn't chase ghosts for a while?"

She smiled softly, curling beside him. "What if we just drove?"

"Where?"

She reached across the bed, grabbed the motel pen, and held it poised above the map.

"Anywhere."

He raised an eyebrow. "You're not going to write *'happily ever after'*, are you?"

Jade tilted her head. "No. That would be her ending."

"Then what?"

She leaned forward, pressed the tip of the pen to the top corner.

And wrote:

Chapter One

Logan blinked. "Chapter one?"

She nodded. "We've been following someone else's ending. It's time we start *our* story."

He smiled—one of the real ones, the kind that made his shoulders drop and his eyes wrinkle just a little at the corners.

Then he leaned in and kissed her.

It wasn't desperate. It wasn't fast.

It was *anchored*.

A quiet answer to a thousand unspoken questions.

When they pulled apart, she rested her forehead against his.

"I don't want to forget this," she whispered.

"You won't," he said. "Because this time—you're the one holding the pen."

Later, when the motel was silent and the desert stretched out like a blank canvas beyond the window, Jade lay awake, tracing the ceiling with her thoughts.

She thought of the Archive.

The mirrors.

The Watcher.

Her father's voice.

And for the first time in weeks, she didn't feel like a character.

She felt like a beginning.

A new page.

A story not yet written—but *finally* hers to tell.

She closed her eyes.

And began.

Chapter 20: The Heart's Treasure

The first light of dawn spilled over the horizon, washing the world in soft shades of rose and gold. They stood on the catwalk of the abandoned observatory, the cool morning air a balm on their bruised and weary bodies. Below them, the distant sound of sirens grew closer, a promise of closure.

Jade held out the map of possibilities she had made for him, its hopeful, imaginary roads a stark contrast to the dark, haunted path that had led them here. "Where to next?" she asked, her voice quiet in the vast morning.

Logan took the map, his fingers tracing the route she'd drawn to the Oregon coast. He looked at the glossy postcard, then at her face, illuminated by the rising sun. He smiled, a slow, sure smile that held all the love in the universe.

"I have a better idea," he said.

He turned the map over, to the blank, unmarked side of her father's old paper. He took the pen from her hand. In the very center, he didn't draw a route or an X. He drew a small, simple square with a door and a window. A house.

"Here," he said, his voice thick with emotion as he tapped the drawing. "We start here. Together."

It wasn't a promise of a destination. It was a promise of a beginning. A home.

Jade's breath caught, a wave of pure, unadulterated joy washing away the last of the ghosts. She leaned in and kissed him, a quiet, perfect kiss that tasted like sunrise and forever. It was the real treasure. It always had been.

One Year Later

The maps looked a little different now.

In the small, sun-drenched house they rented just outside Harmony Creek, the Regret Jar no longer sat on a nightstand. It was on a bookshelf in the living room, a piece of repurposed art. The label now read: *The Hope Jar*. Inside, it was filled not with the folded-up ghosts of the past, but with the bright, colorful slips of a shared future. *Learn to surf. Take a cooking class. Finally visit New Orleans.*

On the wall opposite, a collection of postcards was tacked to a large corkboard. They were real, creased, and stamped, souvenirs from weekend trips to state parks and music festivals. Tucked in a corner, almost as an afterthought, was a faded newspaper clipping. The headline r ead: *Local Man, Silas Blackwood, Sentenced in Kidnapping Plot.* Next to it was a postcard from a bustling city market. The handwriting was his mother's. The note was short: *Thinking of you. Your ship is beautiful out on the open sea. Love, Mom.*

In her small home office, Jade was writing. Not on a secret, anonymous blog, but on a sleek author website with her name proudly displayed at the top: **By Jade Carter**. An email was open on her screen, the subject line glowing: *Book Offer: The Map Between Us.* She smiled and typed out the final words of her story.

That night, they were camped out. Not because they were running, but because they chose to be. They lay in the back of their old Jeep, the doors open to the night, parked in the shady glen by the creek where they had first danced. Her father's original map and the map of possibilities were spread out between them, two parts of the same, single st ory.

"You know," Logan said, his arm wrapped around her as they stared up at the brilliant, starry sky. "My whole life, I was terrified of getting lost."

Jade smiled, resting her head on his shoulder, feeling completely, utterly anchored. "And I," she whispered, "was terrified of being found."

He turned and kissed her, a slow, easy kiss under the stars. They didn't need a map anymore. They were home.

Acknowledgements

Writing *The Map Between Us* has been a journey marked by discovery, detours, and the unexpected beauty that comes from getting a little lost along the way.

To those who inspired the heart of this story — thank you for teaching me that some destinations are people, not places, and that adventure often begins the moment we let go of control.

To my early readers, your belief in these characters and this strange, shifting map of a narrative gave it the oxygen it needed to breathe.

To the writers, dreamers, and artists who reminded me that stories are never truly finished — only paused — thank you for the quiet push forward.

To my family and closest friends: thank you for your patience, your questions, and your unshakable faith in what I was trying to say, even when I hadn't quite found the words yet.

And finally, to the reader holding this book — thank you for choosing to step into this world. I hope you found a piece of yourself along the way.

— Trevor Jensen

About the Author

Trevor Jensen writes stories that explore the thin lines between memory and mystery, truth and myth, the known, romance in many forms, and the unknowable. With a deep love for character-driven journeys and layered emotional landscapes, his novels often blend suspense, romance, introspection, and the quiet magic of human connection.

When he's not writing, Trevor can usually be found walking unfamiliar back roads with a notebook in his pocket, chasing metaphors in secondhand bookstores, or quietly wondering how many maps in life are written backwards.

The Map Between Us is a story close to his heart — one about the stories we inherit, the ones we rewrite, and the people who help us find the way forward.

This is one of many adventures. And the journey continues.

To see more of his publications, please visit the coming-soon web site at:

http://www.TrevorJensenBooks.com